For Quinn—A. N.

For Braydon
and Mason—G. L.

Designed by Winnie Ho

Printed in the United States of America
First Hardcover Edition, May 2016
10 9 8 7 6 5 4 3 2 1
FAC-03427-16078
ISBN 978-1-4847-2585-6
Library of Congress Control Number: 2015949792
Visit www.disneybooks.com

Three Little Words

By Amy Novesky

Illustrated by Grace Lee

Inspired by the Film

DISNEP PRESS
Los Angeles • New York

Hooray! It's a big day!

You're off to sea!

You're on your way!

Wherever you go, whatever you do,

don't forget these three little words . . .

just keep
just **keep**
just keep

swimming!

swimming!

swimming!

When you find yourself swimming alone . . .

just

keep

swimming.

Then just keep swimming.

When you don't know where you're going . . .

keep your head up.

You're bound to run into someone
who can help you.

When you don't know what you're looking for,

just keep swimming . . .

and when you do know . . .

enjoy

the

ride!

When you're surrounded by a bunch
of crabs . . .
don't let them

get

you

down.

When you make a friend . . .

keep

him

forever.

Even the crankiest septopus
has a heart.
Maybe even **three**!

When you discover your Destiny . . .

just keep swimming—beside her.

If you ever

lose your way . . .

just call out to your friends.

When you find yourself

all alone again . . .

don't give up.

don't

give up.

don't give up.

Just

keep

swimming

until you find your way.

You'll soon discover . . .

dreams

come

true.

And when you find what you're looking for . . .

remember those
three little words:
just keep swimming.

just

keep

swimming